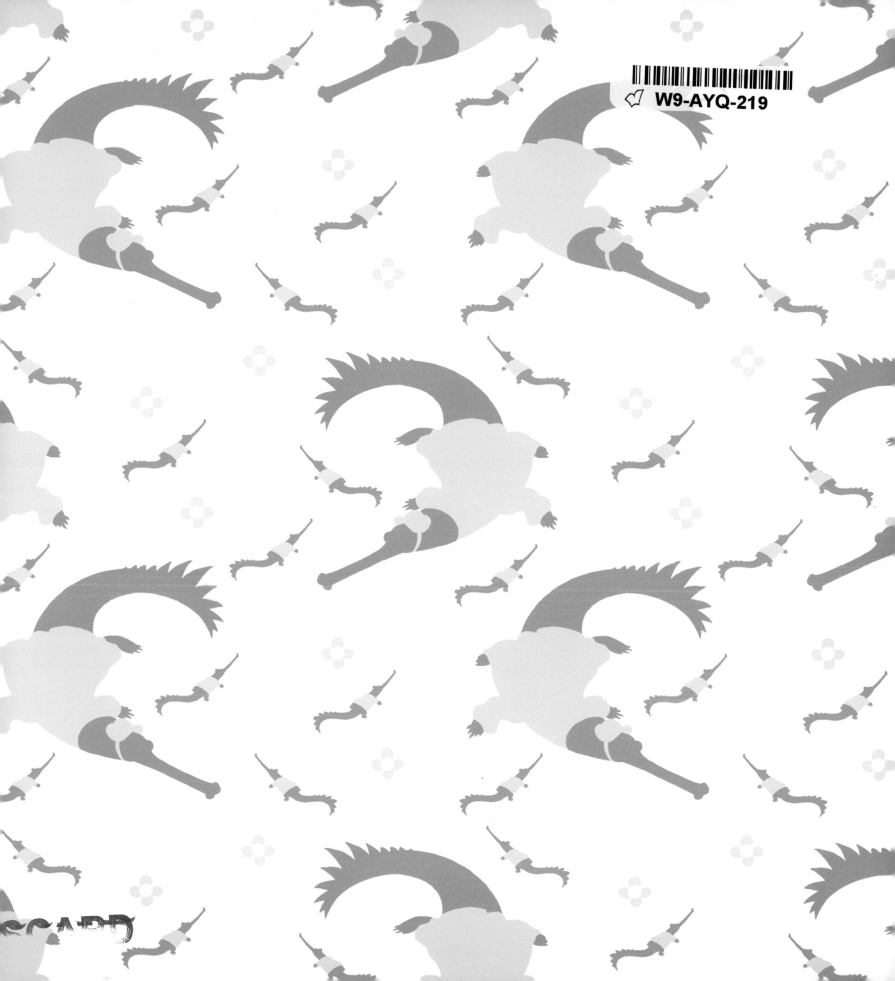

Silver medal winner of
the Key Colors Competition USA, 2020

Key
Colors
Competition

Doris' Dear Delinquents written and illustrated by Emma Ward

ISBN 978-1-60537-690-5

This book was printed in June 2021 at Nikara, M. R. Štefánika 858/25, 963 01 Krupina, Slovakia.

First Edition
10 9 8 7 6 5 4 3 2 1

Clavis Publishing supports the First Amendment and celebrates the right to read.

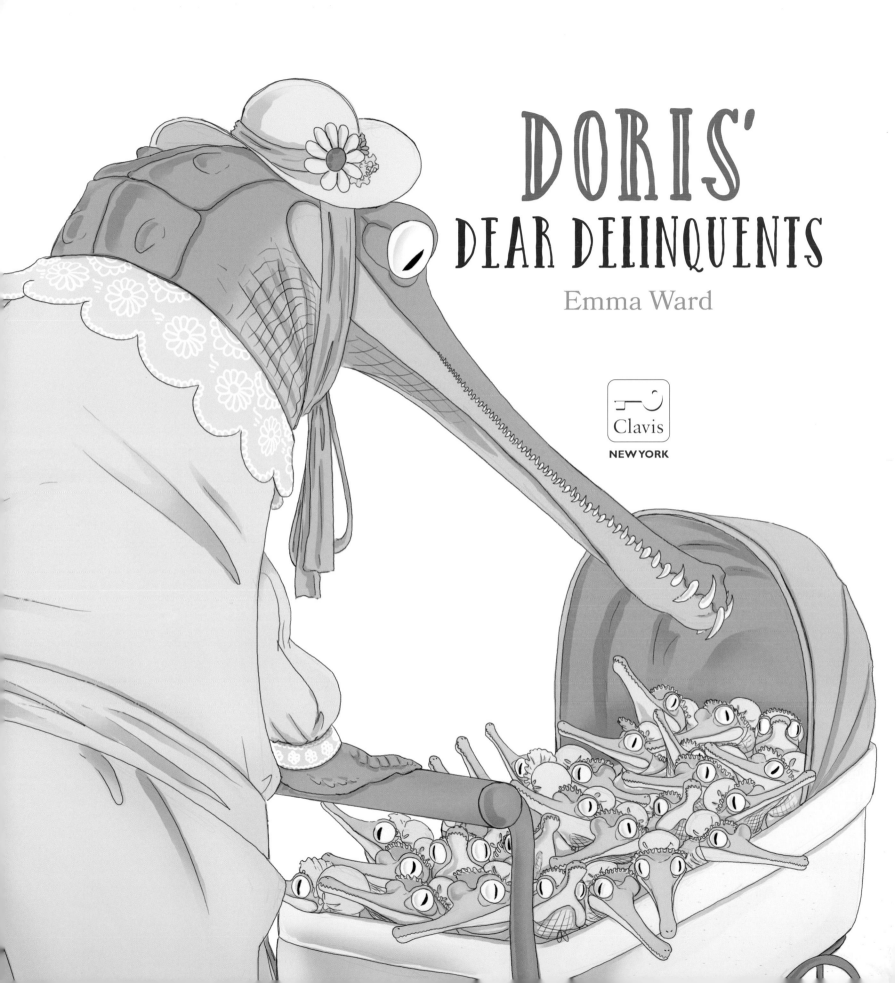

DORIS'
DEAR DELINQUENTS

Emma Ward

Clavis
NEW YORK

One fine day in her modest little home on
the river, DORIS the gharial crocodile became
the proud mother of twenty-six hatchlings.

As they grew older, as all babies do,
they became harder to look after.

AVERY ate the goldfish . . .

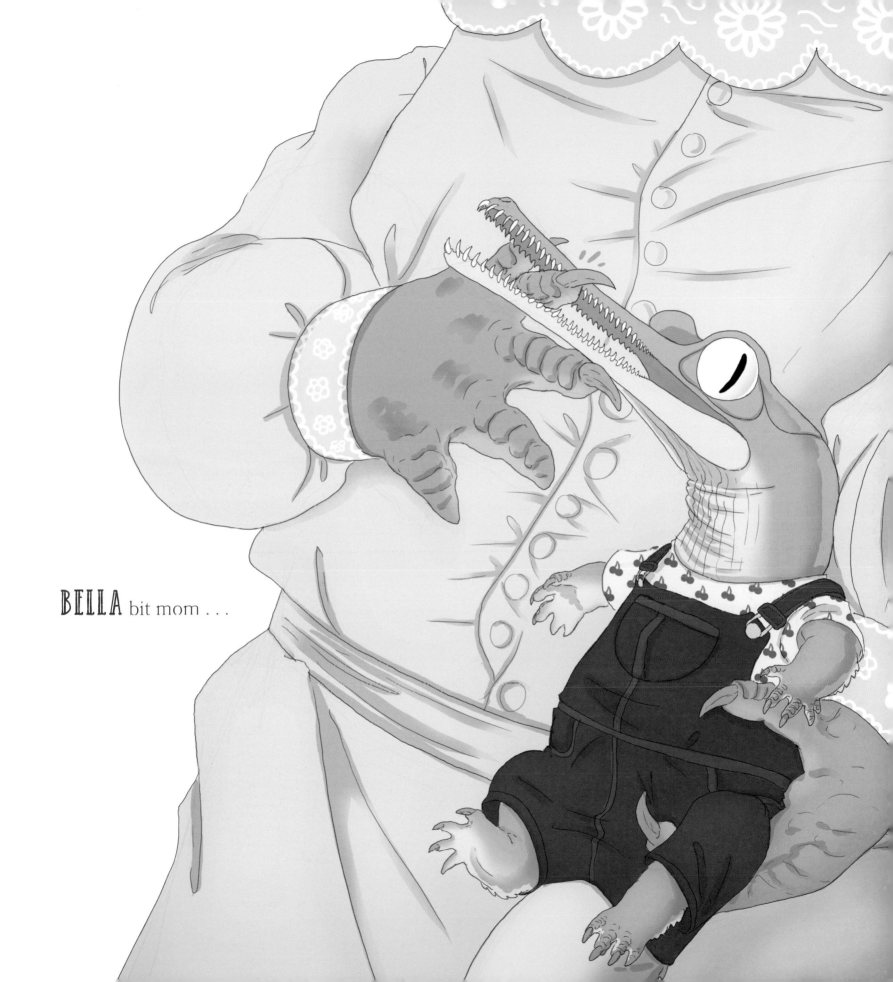

BELLA bit mom . . .

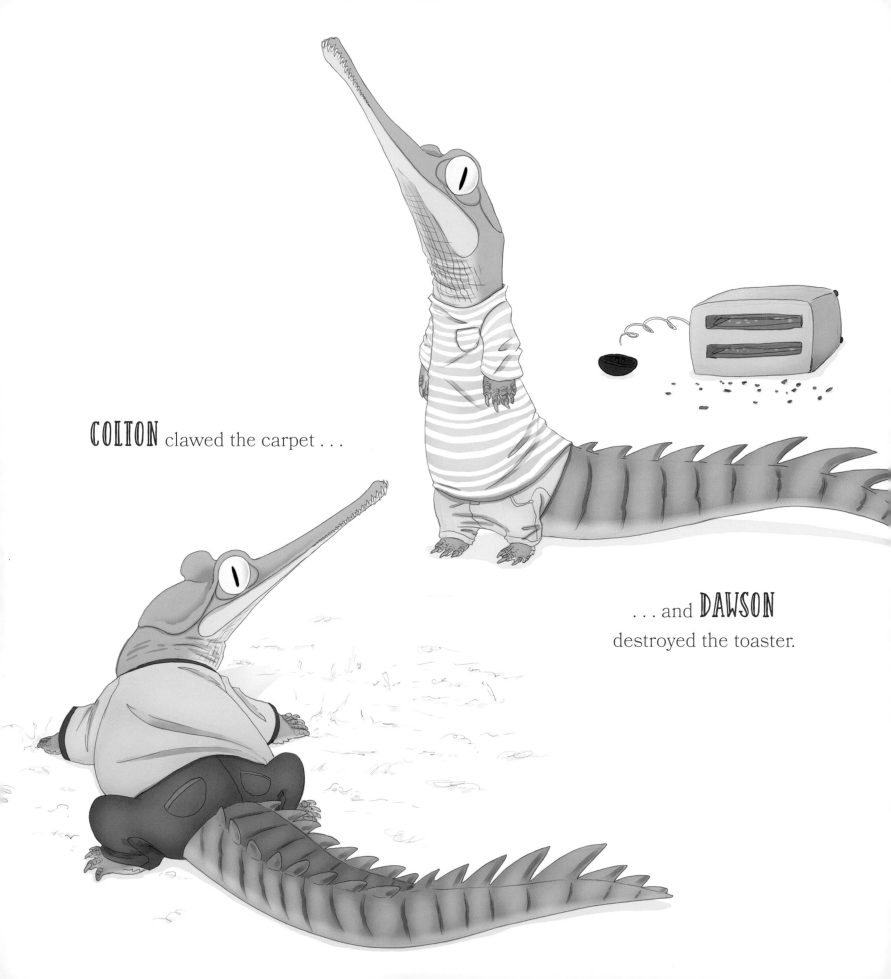

COLTON clawed the carpet . . .

. . . and **DAWSON**
destroyed the toaster.

ELLIE had eaten all of the cookies . . .

FELIX fell down the stairs . . .

GEORGE gorged on the furniture . . .

. . . and **HEATHER** helped.

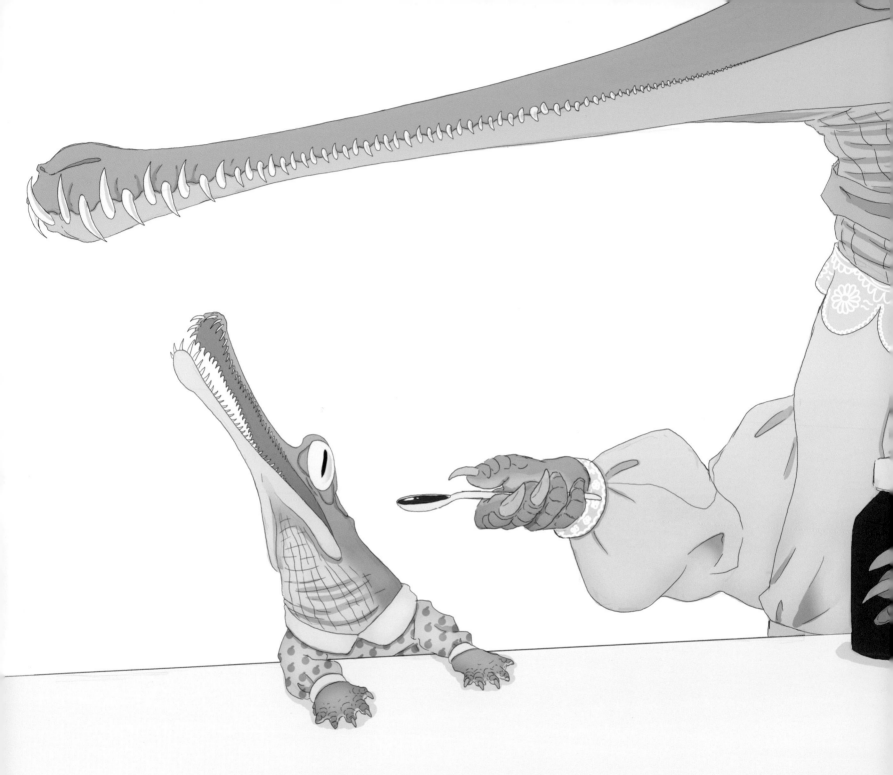

IVY said, "Icky!"

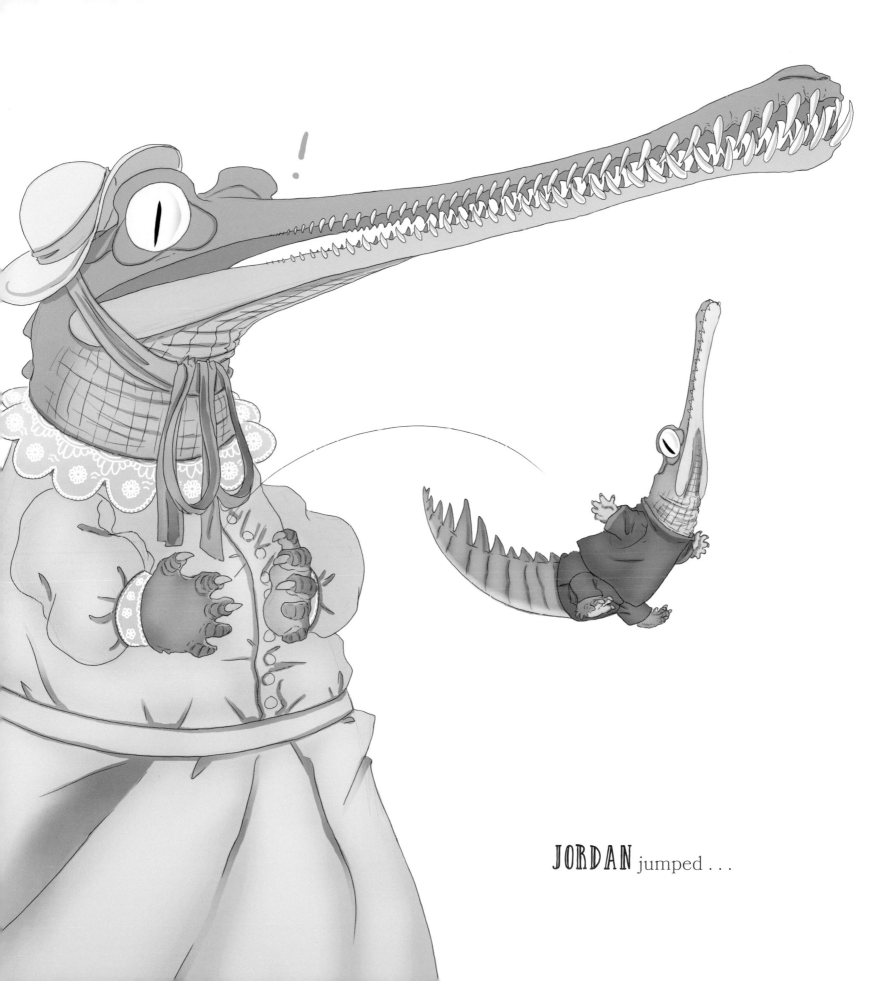

JORDAN jumped . . .

KYLEE kicked . . .

. . . and though DORIS
tried to keep him dressed,
LUCAS lacked his clothes.

MAIA was mean to LUCAS . . .

NICHOLAS was needy . . .

OLIVE had an outburst . . .

. . . and **PENNY** panicked.

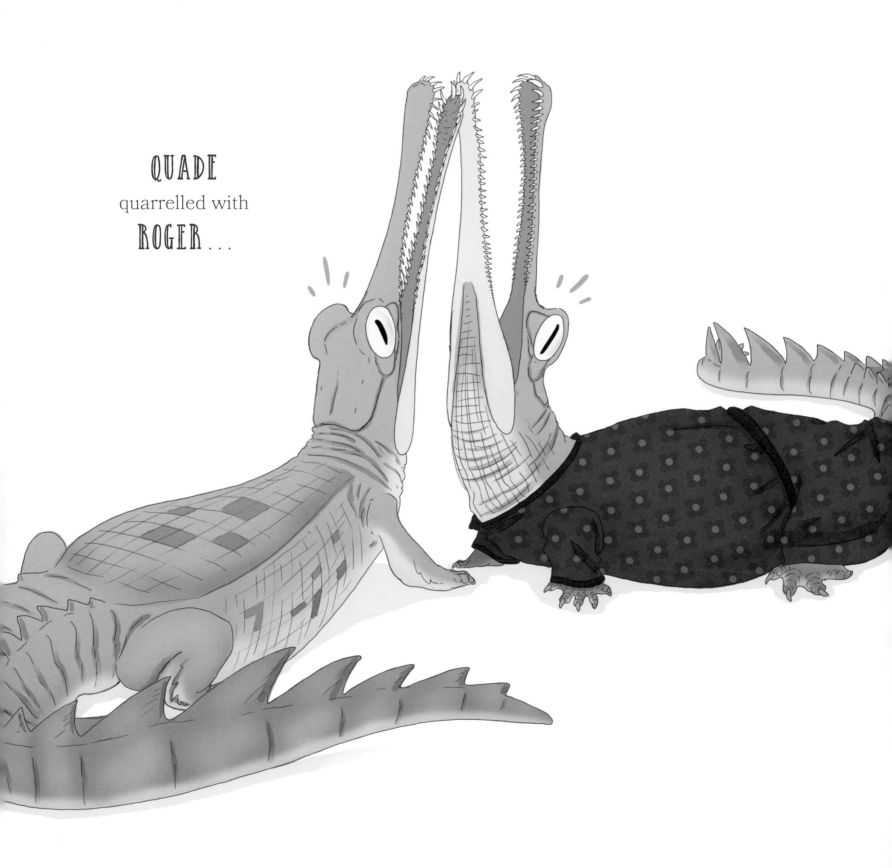

QUADE
quarrelled with
ROGER...

. . . and **ROGER**
refused to wear red.

SAMUEL was sassy . . .

. . . and TABBY tangled the cords.

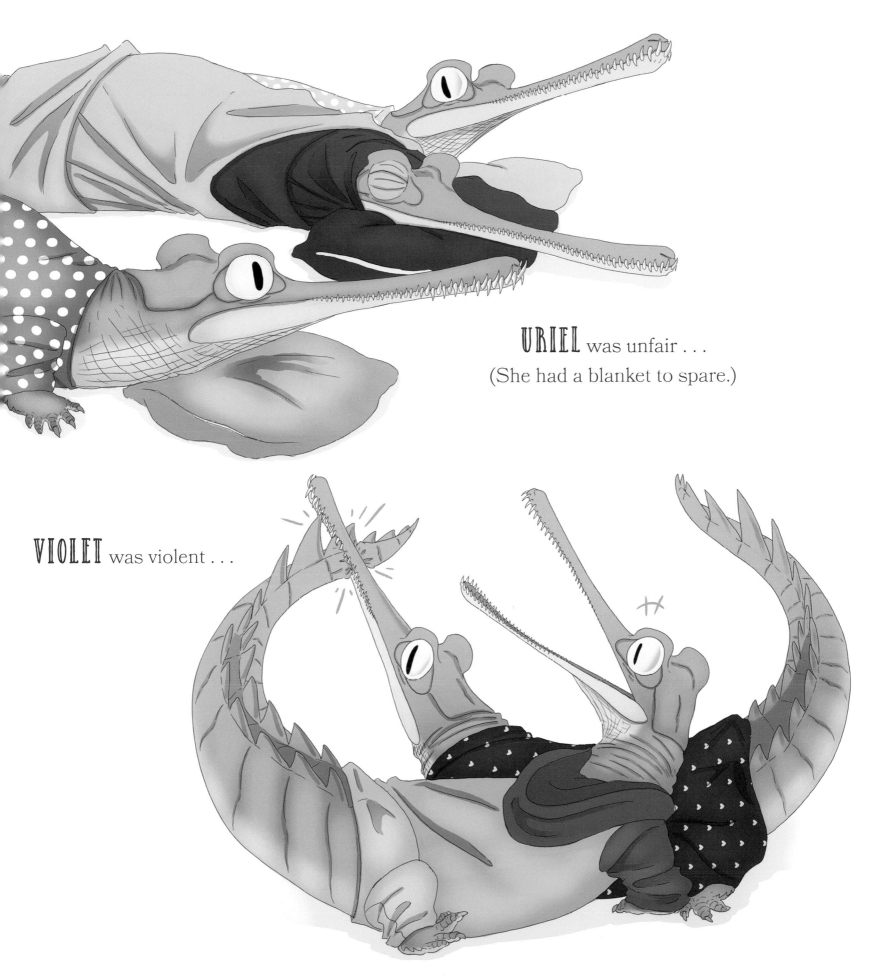

URIEL was unfair . . .
(She had a blanket to spare.)

VIOLET was violent . . .

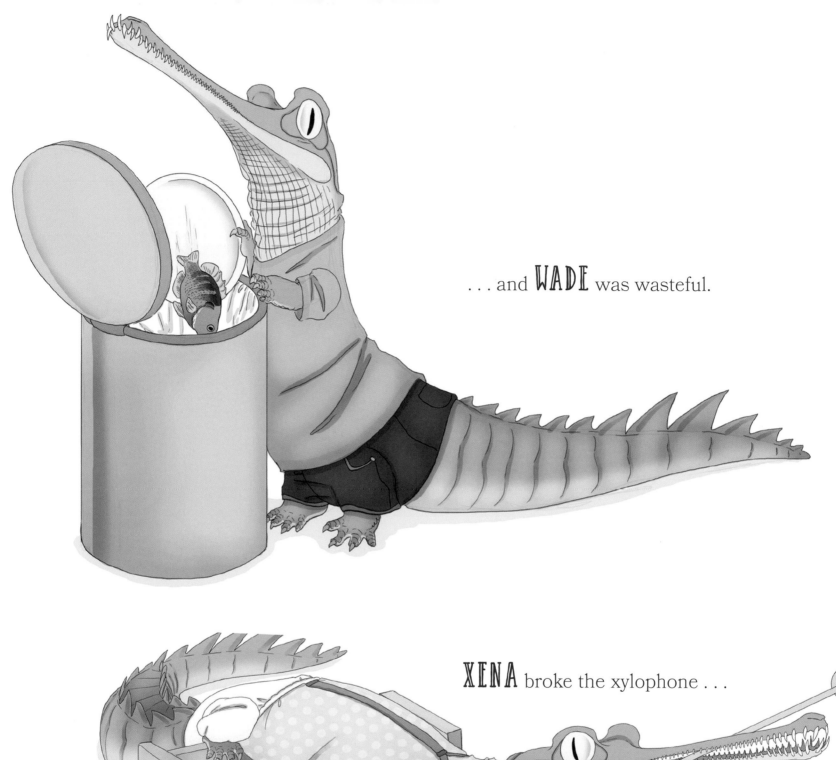

. . . and **WADE** was wasteful.

XENA broke the xylophone . . .

YAEL yanked
on the curtains . . .

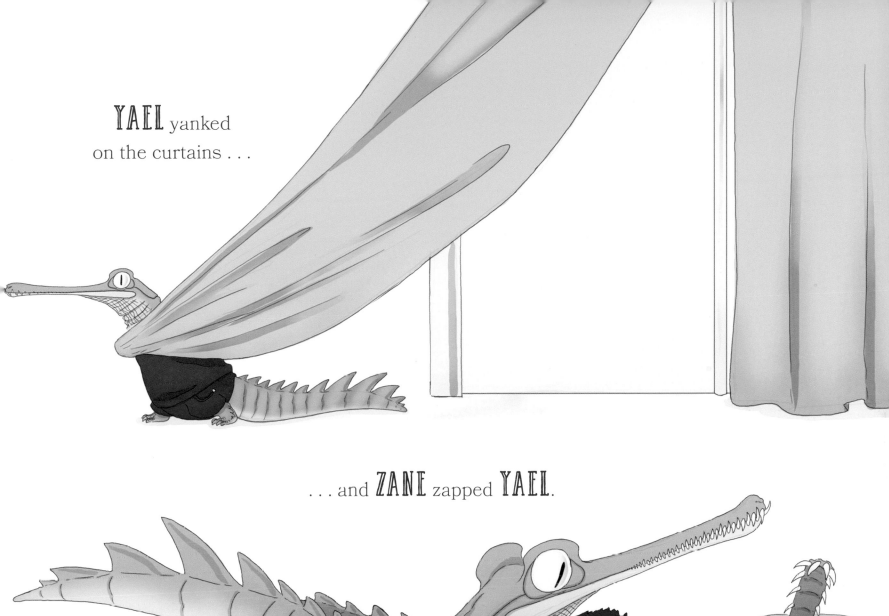

. . . and **ZANE** zapped **YAEL**.

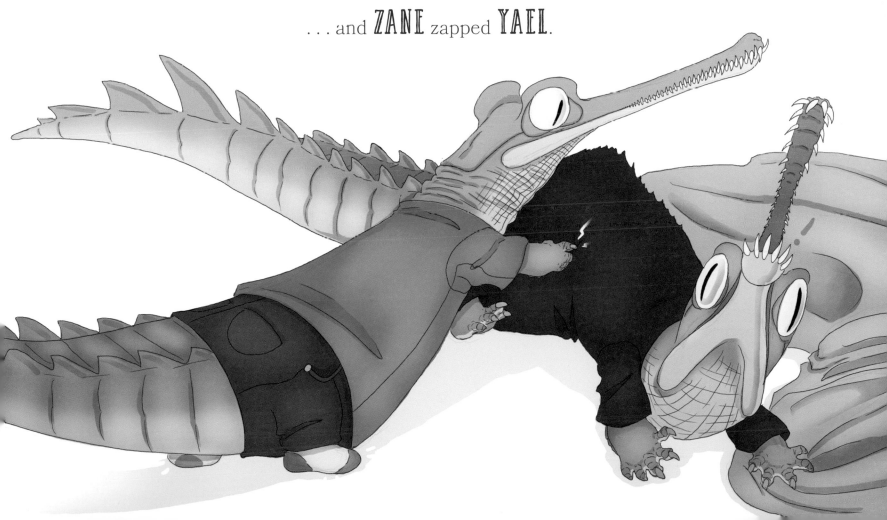

What to do, what to do?
DORIS had something special in mind to make them behave.
They're crocodiles after all.

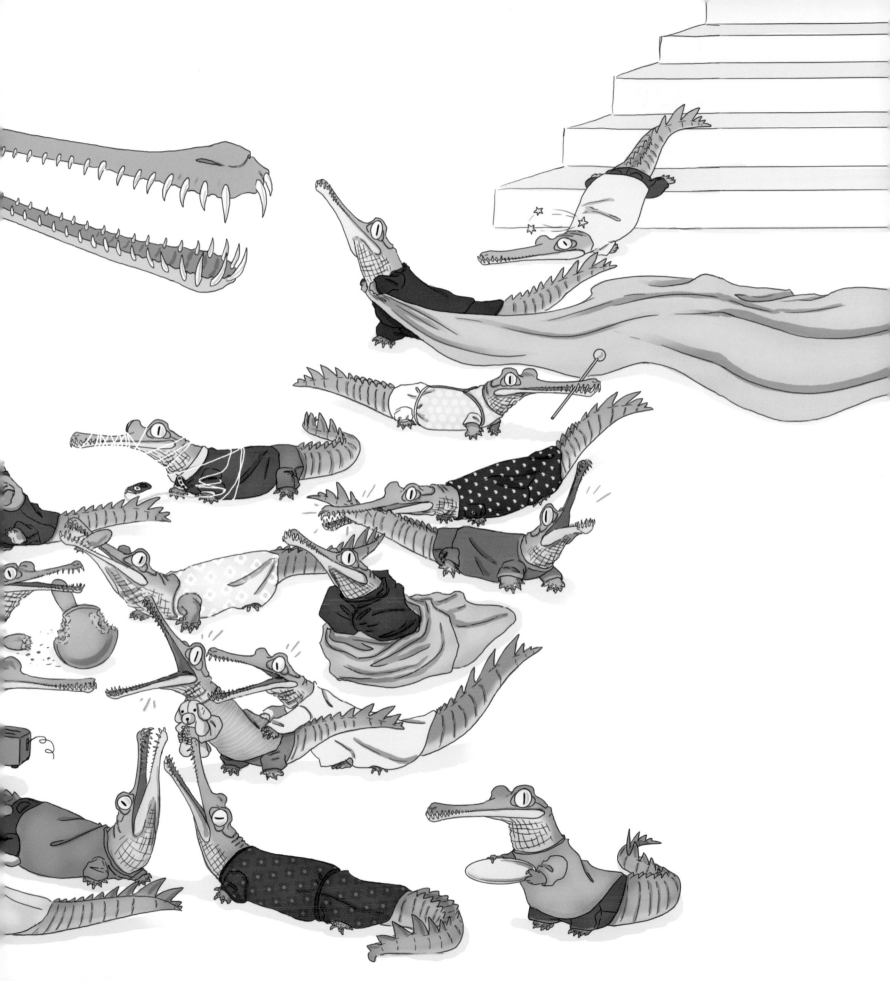

She got **DAD** to take them all for a swim!
So, **DORIS** was able to relax for a short while,
knowing tomorrow would bring
another challenging day.

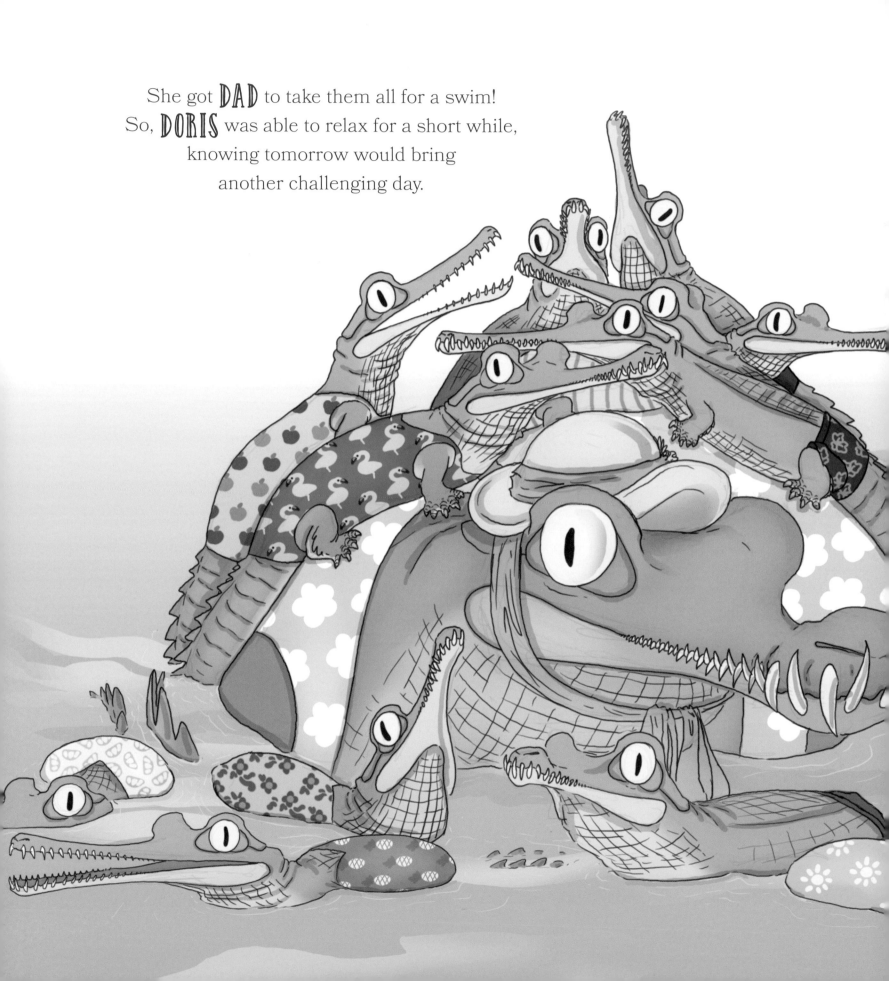

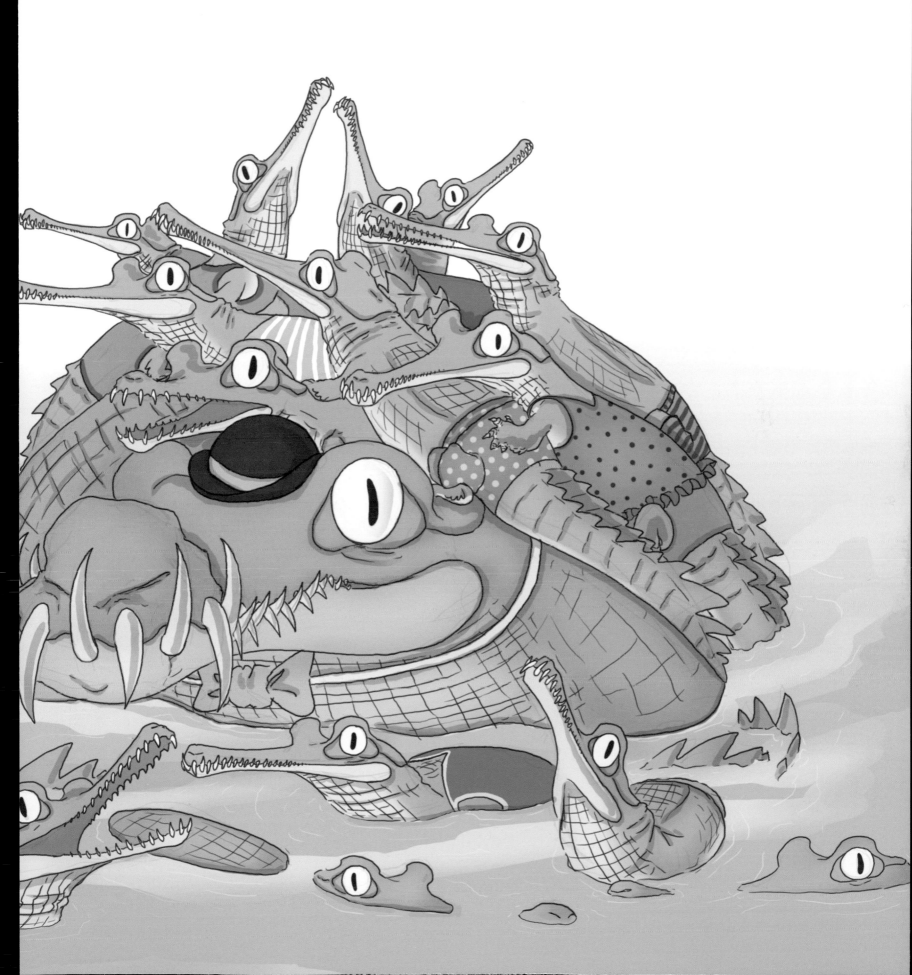